HIS DIRTY SECRET 8

SIDE CHICK CONFESSIONS BOOK 8

MIA BLACK

CHAPTER 1

Jayla

How is this my life? How the fuck is this my life? One second I am watching the senior citizens have a great time, and now I got this crazy bitch screaming in my ear talking about leaving her man alone. Is she talking about Shane? How does she know me? How does she even know where I fucking work? How the fuck did I end up back in drama?

"Leave my man alone!" She now had my arm twisted behind my back while she pushed me against the wall.

"What are you—" I started to ask her but

then from the corner of my eye, I saw one of my coworkers making her way over to us.

"What's going on?" she asked, pulling the crazy bitch off of me. I turned around and the girl tried to take a swing at me, but now there were more people there to separate us.

"Fucking bitch!" she screamed and then left. I watched her go and everything that just happened kept playing over in my head. Was she warning me to stay away from Shane? Or was this a case of mistaken identity?

"Are you okay Jayla?" another coworker asked. "What was that about?"

"I don't know," I told her honestly. "I really don't know. I've never seen that girl before."

"That's crazy."

Work went on. People kept asking me if I was okay and I just nodded my head and told them I was fine. I didn't want them to ask me questions that I didn't have the answer to. I didn't know anything about this chick but she seemed to know a few things about me. One thing for sure was that she knew where I worked. Who was this chick? Was she fucking with Shane? Shane was all about taking it slow when I suggested it, and maybe it was because he had this chick to sleep with while he dated me.

As soon as I got off of work, I called Shane. All the questions that I wanted to know, he had to answer. I was trying to keep calm at work, but the more I thought about it, the more pissed off I got. Was Shane playing me? Had he been lying to me the whole time? What did I really know about him? Did he have more secrets? Shit, did he have more women? For all I knew, this could be one of many women that he was sleeping with. Whatever the case was, I deserved an explanation.

"Hey Jayla, I was just thinking about you?" he said sweetly as he answered my call. He really has no clue about what happened today. Whoever that girl was, she didn't tell him nothing.

"Really?" I took in a deep breath. "I've been thinking about you too. I've been thinking about all this bullshit you've been feeding me. I've been thinking about every little thing you said and now I'm starting to think you are a liar. I told you from the very beginning that I wanted us to be open and honest with each other, but I see I was the only one telling the truth." I was fuming.

"What are you talking about?"

"I'm talking about some crazy chick popping up at my job and telling me to stop messing around with you. She told me that I need to leave you alone."

"What? What is going on? What happened?"

"She told me to stop fucking Shane and then she pushed me against a motherfuckin' wall!" I screamed.

My yells echoed in the parking lot of my job. It wasn't until I saw a car pull out of a parking spot that I realized where I was. I was so into the moment that I had to take a deep breath. I then turned back to my job and saw one of my coworkers outside smoking a cigarette. I went inside my car and closed the door.

"Oh shit." He finally said something.

"I'm done with all of this shit. I'm done with all of it."

"What?"

"I'm done. I'm fucking done Shane!"

"Jayla—"

"No!" I cut him off. "I don't want to hear no bullshit! Your girlfriend came here and made it perfectly clear of what I should do. So I'm going to take her advice."

"That's not my girlfriend."

"Don't tell me that's your wife." I closed my eyes. Not this shit again. I can't be the surprise side chick for the second time in the row.

"No, she's my baby momma."

I was silent. I took a deep breath and yet nothing came out when I opened my mouth. I really tried to speak but I couldn't even form the words.

"Jayla?"

'I'm here." I took in another deep breath. "I'm just trying to backtrack." I closed my eyes. "I'm trying to think about every conversation we ever had and I can't remember you talking about a kid." I paused. "You have a kid?"

"I do."

"And why is this the first time I'm hearing about it? That's usually the first thing a person mentions when they are involved with someone."

"Because I wanted to make sure that we were something serious. I don't just introduce anybody to my child, and on top of that, Damiah isn't the easiest to deal with."

"But to not mention that you have a kid at all? How do you just leave that part out? It's not like you not telling me what your favorite food is; we are talking about your kid!"

"I was going to tell you, but I don't know how to bring up my baby without bringing up my baby mother."

"Why?"

"You've just met Damiah."

I couldn't say nothing else. From that little taste of her, Damiah seems to be crazy as fuck. She actually popped up at my job to fight me.

"But what are you guys? Are you still with her? Are you guys still involved in some way besides the kid? I mean, it wouldn't make sense for her to pop up at my job if there isn't anything going on with you."

"There is nothing going on with us. I know it's going to be hard to believe that considering what happened to you today, but I'm telling the truth. There is nothing going on between me and her, and that's what's pissing her off. She wants me but I don't want nothing to do with her."

"How did she find out about me? How does she even know where I work? Did you mention me to her?"

"Of course not. I don't even know, but I put nothing past her. I won't be surprised if she was following me around and that's how she saw you. Shit, she probably started following you too." He sighed. "I'm sorry though because that's no excuse for her behavior. I also apologize for not giving you a heads up about her. I thought I was protecting you but it turns out I made it worse."

"Well, tell me about her."

"What?"

"Tell me everything about your baby mother. I think after everything she put me through, I deserve to know." I sighed. "And Shane, this time don't leave anything out."

He didn't say anything at first. Maybe he could hear how upset I was, but I didn't care. I just wanted the truth to come out. I hated I had to learn like this, but now I couldn't take no more surprises.

"Let's start from the beginning. Damiah and I were high school sweethearts. We started out as friends and things progressed. We fell in love hard and we helped each other. She went to beauty school, I went to start my businesses, and we had our son three years ago, but something changed. The crazy woman you met today is nothing like the woman that I fell in love with. She was nothing like this. She was nice and easy to be around, but it all changed. I'm still not sure what it was. I'm not sure what happened. For the longest time it bugged me. How could I not see what changed her? Was it something that was always in her? Or did I do something to make it all change? I just knew things were different but I was hoping for the sake of our child that everything would go back to the way it was, but it never did. Finally, something happened and I knew for sure, it was over."

"What happened?"

"She fucked one of my homeboys."

That knocked the wind out of me. I could hear the hurt in his voice as he told me that.

Behind his words, there was pain but it didn't feel like he wanted more from her. It didn't feel like he missed her. When I heard him speak about knowing it was over, it felt final. I didn't know how I knew, but I could feel that he was done and over with her. Just the tone of his voice felt sincere and I knew it was the truth.

"I'm sorry." I felt like apologizing for some reason.

"It's not your fault." He chuckled. "But it seems like ever since that day, she's been crazy. She really thought that we were supposed to stay together after that, but of course that didn't happen. She's snapped and she's just been really obsessed with me."

"I guess." I thought about it. "Still, that bitch came to my job…"

"I'm sorry for that and I will straighten her out...believe that, Jayla. I'm going to handle everything and I just hope that you understand."

As I sat in my car in the parking lot, I did understand what he was saying. He wanted me to still stick around. I thought about all that I went through today with his baby momma, and everything in me was screaming to run away. I just didn't want any drama, and not only did Shane come with drama, but his drama was some bullshit. Did I really want to deal with that shit? Did I really want to have to deal with his baby momma? But even when I thought about leaving, my heart spoke up and it was like I couldn't go. I had feelings for this man and it was not going to suddenly turn off. I wanted it to, but damn, I couldn't help the way I felt about him.

"I hear what you're saying Shane and I feel that you're being honest."

"I am Jayla, I am. I should have told you from the beginning-"

"You don't have to go through the whole apology again; just let me finish." I cut him off. "I understand where you're coming from, but please I'm not going to deal with this bull-shit. I told you that I'm done with the drama and I meant that. You better take care of this and this can never happen again, or I'm done for real"

"I can respect that." He chuckled. "Jayla, I'm going to make sure this never happens again."

The phone call ended there. I started my car engine and finally drove away from work. My head was still swimming after everything, but my heart felt sure. My heart knew what it wanted but letting my heart make the important decisions had gotten me in trouble before. So I was going to give Shane a chance, but until he fixed the situation, I was going to make sure I didn't fall for him too hard. I was not about to have another situation like I did with Darius.

"No more drama," I promised myself.

Shane

"Fuck!" I cursed out loud in the gym's office. I've been holding on to all my anger until I got off the phone with Jayla. I didn't want her to know how pissed I was, but now that the conversation was over, all the rage inside of me just came out. How could Damiah do this? By attacking Jayla, she was making things for Jayla and me more difficult. I couldn't let Damiah get away with this.

"Marlene." I left the office and I went out to the gym floor. This new gym just opened up and it was almost full of people. I had to look past the gym goers and saw the manager of this gym. I found her speaking with some new customers and when she finished, she came straight to me.

"I just got those two to not only sign up for a monthly membership, but they are bringing their Bible study people here too. That is like ten new memberships in one day. We have blown past our goal and it's not even a month since the grand opening." She smiled. This should have been good news for me, but right now I didn't want to hear nothing really. I just wanted to go straighten out Damiah.

"That's great." I forced a smile though because Marlene didn't need to know my personal problems. "Hey, I'm going to be leaving. The overnight manager is going to be here a little bit early. I was going to show him around the gym because he's fairly new. Would you mind showing him the ropes?"

"Not a problem," she assured me. "I have a full staff here, so everything should be fine."

"Thanks."

I left before she could even say anything more. I got in my car and whipped out of the parking lot so fast. Racing to Damiah's, all I saw was red. In my head I heard Jayla telling me that she wanted no more drama. I heard her warnings and I knew she was serious. I always took what Jayla said seriously. She carried herself differently than Damiah. When she told me from the beginning that we were to keep things honest, I wanted to tell her about my kid then, but I knew I would have to explain Damiah. Fucking Damiah.

I got to her place and ran up the steps.

"Damiah!" I banged on her front door. "Damiah, open this fucking door!" I ordered. There was a little bit of noise on the other side of the door. It got silent again and I banged on the door one more time. "Damiah! I'm not playing games with you! Come and open this fucking door." Suddenly, the door swung open.

"What?!" She said with all the attitude in the world but with no sense at all. I stormed right in the house.

"You know why the fuck I'm here Damiah." I looked her in the eyes as I spoke. She just shook her head, rolled her eyes, and went to close the door.

"Fuck that bitch!" she yelled. "She needed to know who the fuck I am and she needed to know her place. That bitch needed to know that I'm here and I'm here to motherfuckin' stay."

This was the crazy shit I was talking about. Damiah lived in this altered sense of reality. I could tell that she seriously thought that what she did was okay.

"Damiah, we are not together!" I made sure she heard me even though I was stating the obvious. "We are never going to be together! Get that shit through your thick fucking skull! What you and I had is over and it's been over."

"How can you say that? We have a son together! I am the mother of your child! "

"And that's all you'll ever fucking be to me. We are not friends, we are not buddies, and we are never going to be together, Damiah. That shit is done and over with."

"No, it's not. You are never going to be with another woman like me and you're never going to love another woman like me. You are never going to have another chick like me!" Her eyes looked deranged. There was something seriously off about this chick.

"You really think that you're all that I have. That is over and done with. Don't stand there and look crazy. You killed this relationship when you fucked my homeboy." I threw the truth right back in her face. "Once you fucked him, you ended us...permanently."

"Whatever." She tried to dismiss the entire conversation, but I wasn't having it.

"No, this is how it is Damiah. Leave my girl alone." She spun around and looked at me like I had ten heads.

"Yo' girl?"

Something came over her eyes again. They looked more deranged than before. She kept looking at me as if she wanted me to take back what I said, but I wasn't budging.

"Yeah, that's my girl. Mess with her again and see what happens, Damiah. Leave her alone and stay the fuck in your lane."

"My lane?"

"You heard me, Damiah. Know your place. You are not my girl, you are not my wife, you not even my fucking side chick. Be a mother to our child and that's all you got to fucking do."

"Who the fuck do you think you're talking to?" She got in my face. "You said that we were going to be together forever. I'm just making sure you keep your promise." She kept bringing up the past and surely didn't hear what I told her before.

"Get the fuck out of here with that nonsense, Damiah."

"No, fuck you!" she screamed. "You and the fucking bullshit that you're trying to put me through. I'm not going anywhere, Shane! I am here to fucking stay! I am going to be your wife! I am going to be with you forever! So fuck that little bitch that you with. If I got to kick her ass a thousand times then so be it! At the end of all of this, it's going to be you and me together forever...like we planned." She screamed with her hands in my face. She was flailing and going crazy. She kept yelling, shouting, and throwing her hands in my face....and I snapped.

My hands were around her neck so fast that it wasn't even a thought. I pushed her hard against the wall. Her eyes opened wide and I was breathing heavily. I could feel my nostrils flaring and my chest moving up and down. My whole body felt hot and I didn't really feel like myself. I leaned close to her ear.

"You leave her the fuck alone, Damiah. This ain't me asking you, I'm tellin' yo' ass what you're going to do or my son will be growing up without his mother. Do you understand?" I threatened. I looked back at her face and in her eyes I knew she was about to say something smart. I gripped a little tighter. "Do you understand?" I repeated. She nodded her head and I let her go.

Damiah fell to the floor and started to gasp for air. She was trying to breathe and I hated myself for getting this angry. She was the only person that could make me get like this. I looked at her and when she locked eyes with me, I shook my head.

"Don't make me have to come back here, Damiah. I'm not going to tell you this again; next time I won't be so nice and let your ass go." I could barely stand the sight of her. I turned and walked out the house.

～

Damiah

AFTER HE SLAMMED MY DOOR, I got up and locked it. I started taking deep breaths. It really hit me that this nigga had his hands around my throat. When he grabbed my neck, I thought that he was just going to hold me, but he seriously started to squeeze my fucking neck. He did all of that shit over that stupid bitch! Shane could be so sweet and so nice, but when he got mad…

I went to the bathroom and splashed some cold water on my face. I looked in the mirror and l saw his handprints on my neck. I got something for that ass. He really thought that he could put his fucking hands on me and I was going to let that shit go? He got me all the way fucked up if he thought that I was going to let that shit slide. I started laughing and smiling because Shane really thought that he could be the only one that's crazy. He must have forgot that I was crazy as fuck too.

"Okay Shane, that's how you want to do it," I said, looking at the bruises on my neck with a smirk on my face. "I'm going to fall back on that dumb ass bitch you with…for now. I'm going to make you think that shit is all good and well. I'm going to act like everything is cool, and then I'm going to have to what I have to do. I'm going to do whatever I need to do to get my family back; I can promise you that."

CHAPTER 2

Jayla

The stares at my job had finally stopped. Three weeks ago when Shane's crazy ass baby mother popped up at my job and went ape shit, everyone stared at me. They kept looking and talking behind my back. For three weeks, most of my coworkers and even some of the patients kept asking me if I was okay. I faked a smile and told them I was. It was embarrassing to have this happen to me, especially at work. Luckily now, all that seemed to have died down. Work was retuning back to normal and it was all behind me.

For the first few days after the crazy bitch

popped up, I was looking over my shoulder, but after Shane told me that he shut it down, I'd felt better. It was nice to know that Shane was a man of his word, because I hadn't seen her at all. Shane had been taking me out almost every night these past three weeks. I knew it was mostly because of how we felt about each other, but I knew a part of him felt guilty. He was always showing me way of how sorry he was for what his baby mother did to me, and I appreciated it. But as much as I liked him, there was something holding me back from him. I just couldn't let myself fall all the way for him.

"Hey girl!" Samara said to me while I was clocking out of work.

"Oh, hey stranger." I winked at her. "I haven't really seen you," I pointed out. "It's been a while."

"Yeah, I know. My schedule changed because I was helping others cover their shifts." She sighed as she clocked out. "Besides, you've been pretty busy yourself." She gave me a knowing look. I shook my head because I knew what she was getting at. I hadn't been seeing much of Samara lately and maybe it was because I was spending a lot of my free time with her brother. "How about we hang out tonight?" she suggested. "We can go have some drinks, dress up sexy, and just have fun. Plus today at work was so crazy, we could use a drink...or five."

"Damn girl, five drinks?" I laughed.

"You're right; we should have six," she said and we both busted out laughing.

As soon as I got home, I started to get ready for my girl's night out with Samara. I hopped in the shower, chose an outfit, and completely changed. My whole look was complete. I was wearing a nice all black romper. I threw on some cute silver high heeled sandals to go with it. Taking out my phone, I requested an Uber while I headed towards the kitchen. Keon wasn't around which meant he was either at class or hanging out with Crystal. I went in my purse and threw down some money on the counter. I knew they were going to be hungry and I couldn't chance Keon burning down my house because he wanted to attempt to cook. The Uber driver called me two minutes after that and I was out the door.

It didn't take too long for my ride to pull up to the bar. I was there and immediately I spotted Samara. She was wearing this backless red dress. I saw some guys making eyes at her, which was no surprise, but to see her smile at them was weird. Samara never gave these guys the time of day. She was so loyal to her man that was locked up.

"Hey." I came up to her and she greeted me with a hug. "What you doing?" I cut eyes at her.

"Just giving these thirsty ass dudes a little bit of attention." She rolled her eyes. She then looked me up and down. "Bitch, I could kill you. Why you got to show out like that?" she joked.

"Oh this little ole thing?" I winked.

"Whatever," she laughed. "I'm ready to start drinking."

We sat down at the bar, talking about work and how crazy it was. The patients weren't so bad, but the new supervisor was driving us crazy. She was trying to be lay down these stupid ass rules and no one was following them. It wasn't before long that the director had to put her in her place. It was just a long day of petty arguments and people trying to walk on eggshells.

"Can you believe that she tried to come in there and run the place like it was the army?" Samara asked. "You'd think she was G.I Joe or something." She took a sip of her wine. "More like G.I Hoe," she went on and I almost choked on my drink.

"What? What makes you say that?"

"I saw the way she was looking at Mr. Scott."

"Samara, he's like 89 years old."

"I know, and I said what I said." She winked.

I laughed and ordered some more mozzarella sticks.

"It's so nice to hang out with you." Samara smiled. "I haven't seen much of you."

"I know, it's been pretty hectic."

"Honestly, I thought you were avoiding me."

"Avoiding you? Why would I do that?"

"Because I didn't warn you about my brother's crazy ass baby momma."

"Right." I nodded and took a sip when I heard about that crazy bitch. I was trying to get away from anything that reminded me of her and now, here I was talking about her.

"I didn't mean to purposely leave her out, but there are some things about me and Shane's past that are only for Shane to share."

"What do you mean? Is there more about his baby momma that I should know?"

"No, I know my brother would be upfront and honest about that when the time is right," she clarified. "It's just that, there's a lot you should know about Shane and I. Some of the stories are for only Shane to tell you."

"And what about the rest? Is there anything you can tell me now?"

The shine in Samara's eyes faded just a bit when I asked her that. She was smiling the whole time but now, she stopped. I could feel the story just weighing on her.

"Shane and I didn't exactly have a great childhood. We had it rough." She sighed. "You see, we grew up in the projects so we didn't have much and we had to be tough soon. There was no time for us to be shy or soft in the hood. If we were soft, we would have been taken advantage of. Shane was very overprotective of me and it makes sense, because the neighborhood was really…. you know." I nodded because I knew what she meant.

"I remember one time when I was walking home and I was going up the stairs and some guy just grabbed me. He pulled my leg and tried to pull me down. I was so lucky because my brother came and just kicked his ass. It was so much."

"I can imagine."

"And on top of all that we had that typical hood shit. You know what I mean." She took a long sip from her drink. "One of my uncles was a crackhead and yes, he stole shit. He took anything that wasn't nailed down. I remember my godmother who lived down South sent me some beautiful gold hoop earrings. Jayla, you know the ones that Jennifer Lopez had back in the day? I had those exact same ones. She even sent me some diamond earrings. So you can guess what he did."

"He stole them?"

"And then he pawned them."

"That's fucked up."

"Well, he dead now." She looked away.

There was pain in her voice and she was

barely looking at me. She took in another deep breath.

"So, I think it was the way we grew up is what changed Shane."

"What do you mean changed?" I asked.

"He just decided that enough was enough. He wasn't going to be living like that anymore. There was just too many fights and a lot of bullshit. My mother was on pills so she wouldn't have to deal with the nonsense, so it was basically just me and him. He would wake me up for school, walk me to school, walk me from school. He was that someone who watched over me, made sure that I was okay. He was more than my brother, he was my guardian. I owe a lot to my brother." She got choked up once again.

Samara stopped and smiled. She took in a deep breath and I could tell that talking about the past brought back a lot of memories.

"He's done a lot," I commented. "He sounds like a great man."

"He is." She sipped on her drink. "I don't know what my life would have been like without my brother." I nodded my head but I was feeling joy on the inside. Shane was a good man. I knew what it was like to grow up in a certain environment where you basically have to raise yourself and your siblings.

"I guess that's why he worked so hard to become successful," I added.

"Yes. My brother and I caught a lot of shit when we were growing up. Not only with our family members basically abandoning us, but people just made fun of us. We didn't have the latest clothes, or the best shoes, and you know how can kids can be. Kids can be really mean sometimes."

"Kids can be assholes," I corrected her, remembering my own childhood.

"Right," she agreed. "So he bust his ass to make sure we were alright. You know he worked a lot of jobs when we were growing up. Nothing steady, but he did things here and there to get us clothes, a place to sleep, just provide from him and I. I think that's why as much money as he makes, he's not a jerk."

"Yeah, he doesn't seem that way. He's a very humble person. He's never come across as flashy with his money."

Samara went to talk more about Shane. I guessed with a little liquid courage, she felt like she could open up more to me. It was nice to hear about all the good deeds Shane did for her. In a lot of ways, Shane reminded me of myself and all the sacrifices and hard work I did for my brother and sister. I wanted to make sure they had a great life. With one sister in college on a scholarship and with Keon's life making a complete turnaround, I got to say I was a little proud of myself. Maybe that was the connection that was keeping me around with Shane. Maybe that was what was keeping me close to him, and I didn't mind that at all.

"So, what is new with you?" I asked her.

"Nothing really." She shrugged. "I'm just a working mom and that's it."

"Oh, come on. There is more to you than that. You are not only a mom, you're a woman."

"A woman who's man is in prison for what seems like to be forever." She sighed.

"Are you okay? For the first time it sounds like you're tired."

"I love my baby father with all my heart. He's the love of my life, but I'd be lying if I said it was easy to be out here alone while he's serving time. It's hard. It gets really lonely. His letters and his cards, and all the things that he could send me are nice, but when I'm all alone...it's hard."

"I can't even imagine." I looked at her. Her shoulders were slumped and she was stirring her drink with her straw. "It'll get easier."

"I know that Jayla, and I don't want you to worry about me. It's just one of those days." She sighed.

"The days when you really miss your man."

"And his dick." She gave me a wicked smile.

I laughed. Only Samara could turn a situation around with a few words. We started joking, laughing, and talking about all the crazy things that we've seen. We kept eating and having a great time together. When the night for us was ending, we shared an Uber and I made sure she got home safe. After my ride got me home, I got ready for bed. I changed my clothes and climbed into bed. As I laid there, I looked up at the ceiling. The sounds of the cars driving outside, Keon's tv turned on, and even the fridge all faded away as I thought about Shane. He was becoming more than just a good looking rich guy to me. There was so much more about him that I wanted to learn and that could only happen if I opened up more to him.

CHAPTER 3

Jayla

"How is it that you look more beautiful every time I see you?" Shane smiled at me as I stepped out my house.

"You say that all the time." I blushed.

"And I'll stop saying it the second it's not true, but I just don't see that happening." His blazer fit him so well and went with his slacks.

"Here I thought I was going to be over-dressed." I was wearing a royal blue dress. It was backless, but still elegant. I pulled my hair up into a bun and wore diamond stud earrings.

"You look great as always." He took my

hand, flipped it over, and kissed my palm. He sent tingles all the way down my spine. I kept all my excitement to myself.

"So, where are we going?"

"It's a surprise."

"It's always a surprise," I giggled. "How about for once we switch it up and you tell me where we're going?"

"Where's the fun in that?"

We got in his car and we were off. When we stopped in front of this restaurant I looked over at him.

"You could have just said that we were going to eat."

"And again I say, where's the fun in that?" He chuckled. He took my hand and led me inside.

The whole place was so beautiful and glamorous. Once again, Shane took me to this breathless place. He was showing me the beauty of Houston, Texas. I smiled to myself at how a nice gentleman he really was. He spoke to the maitre'd and we were seated. When we sat down, a waiter greeted us and took our order for drinks. I wanted to be clear headed tonight so I just ordered a virgin drink and he did the same. I looked around and it felt like I was in Italy. The restaurant did a great job decorating it.

"What are you looking at?" he asked me as I glanced around.

"The restaurant," I admitted. "It's so gorgeous here." I looked up at the ceiling. "Oh my gosh, are those little angels?" I asked.

"Yeah, they really wanted people to get the feel of Italy."

"They did."

"I'm so glad you came out here with me tonight."

"Of course I did Shane. Why wouldn't I have come out tonight?"

"Because of all the drama with my baby momma," he told me flat out.

"I'm glad you brought it up."

Just then the waiter came with our drinks. We ordered our food and after he left, I could feel Shane's eyes looking right at me.

"Well?"

"I've been through a lot before you. I know I've said it again and again, but I just want to make sure that you know it. I want to make sure you know that when at times I feel guarded that it has nothing to do with you, it's all about me. As much as I'm feelin' you, I have to make sure that I am alright and that I don't get hurt."

"I understand that."

"I'm glad that you do, because I think that you and I could be something great. I think that you and I could be something, but I just have to take my time. I don't want to rush into it all crazy, especially with the whole thing with you baby momma."

"Trust me I get it Jayla. I get it more than you know"

The food came right on time and as hungry as I was, I was more curious about what Shane meant.

"This looks so good." His eyes were almost lusting after his lasagna.

"What did you mean?" I cut straight to the chase.

"I mean that I want to eat this food." He looked at me like I was crazy.

"No," I giggled. "I meant, what did you mean about what I said before. It sounds like you had more to say and then our food came."

"Jayla..." He started and then he stopped.

"Go ahead." I encouraged him. "I can take it." I smiled.

"Jayla, I know I've told you about my situation. I've told you how me and her broke up, but after that whole thing it's been a lot of drama. I know how you feel about drama and I know you want to avoid it, but I can't. I love my son and I want to be a part of his life, and in order for that to happen, I have to deal with her and her bullshit." He sighed. I slowly nodded my head. I got what he was saying. He was telling more of the truth about his situation and I appreciated it, but it was a lot.

"That's…. something," was all I could manage to say.

"I can see that you're kind of apprehensive with me and I understand it. No one wants to go into any relationship knowing for sure that there is going to be drama, but I can promise you that I will do my best to keep that away from you."

"Well I haven't seen her since so I know that's true."

"And you won't," he said firmly. "When it came to you, I told her that I wasn't taking any of her nonsense. I know this might be much but I hope it isn't a dealbreaker with you."

I thought about it. I did not want any drama, especially after the whole bullshit that I dealt with back in Atlanta, but looking at Shane being honest with me, it just made me like him even more. He could have easily lied about the situation and I wouldn't know any better, but he was honest. Between what Samara told me about him and how he was here with me, I was falling for him a bit more. It was a great but very scary feeling.

"Despite what's happened to me in Georgia, I'm not really use to dealing with baby mother's." I explained. "I mean, I have heard and seen all these types of stories and I just never thought I would have to deal with it. I never thought I would date a guy with a kid to be honest from all the stories that I heard."

"I know and I appreciate you for telling me that. I wish my situation was different. I wish she was cool and nice and that we all could get along. That's my goal though. I want it to be peaceful, but I can't be the only one that wants that. I will do my best to keep the drama away from you...and us. I think the fact that we both want to take it slow is perfect."

"I agree."

The rest of the dinner went smoothly. He went on to talk about how beautiful I was and how happy he was that I was giving him my time. He was so sincere with his words and he knew how to make me feel special. After dinner, he drove me home and we stood in front of my door. Parts of me wanted me to bring him inside, but I knew it was best to just leave things out here.

"Thank you for tonight." I hugged him and breathed him in. I felt myself want him but I couldn't give in.

"My pleasure." He kissed my forehead and then went back to his car. I watched him drive away before I went inside.

Shane

PULLING my car to my home, I stopped short when I noticed Tone's car in my driveway. I completely forgot that he was crashing with me while he got his floors done in his new place. He always wanted his home to look picture perfect, but right now I just needed some time to myself. After leaving my date with Jayla, my mind was racing.

"Yo!" Tone greeted me as soon as I stepped in my place. He was sitting on my couch watching some soccer game on the big screen.

"I didn't know you watched soccer." I gave him a dap.

"I watch all sports, even sumo wrestlers, my nigga," he joked and I started cracking up. Even though I started out wanting to be alone, it was nothing like hanging out with my boy, Tone.

"What's up? What you doing?"

"I should be asking you that question. Shouldn't you be in some pussy right now? I thought you had this date with Jayla."

"I did go out with Jayla."

"And I'm guessing you still didn't get your dick wet?"

"You are very vulgar today," I laughed as I went to grab a beer from my fridge.

"I'm sorry, but you been dating this girl for so long and not fucking her. I just don't get it."

"That's because you never met anyone like Jayla."

I took a long swig from the beer. Tone stood up and I tossed him a beer.

"Listen, you know you my boy and I got your back for whatever."

"Yes…" I said suspiciously. "Where are you going with this?"

"I'm just saying that I got your back but I'm not looking for a girl right now. I'm trying to stay focused on this money and on the business."

"And you don't have women lined up?"

"I do, but I'm just having fun."

"Fun?"

"Yes, fun. We are making crazy money, our businesses are doing well, why would I want to settle down? I'm in my prime!" He laughed.

"Alright keep talking like that and you're going to be that old guy in the club."

"Good, that way I can get all the young thots." He smiled and we both laughed.

Tone had always been this crazy. He loved

having all the ladies and it had never distracted him from the business. He had always had his head in the business. With him, the gyms had expanded to places that I never thought possible.

"So, what's up with the business? Are we happy with all these locations?" I asked him as I fell to the couch.

"They are all making money, but some of them have the same problems."

"What is it?"

"Parking. One of the things I think we have to do is look for a parking lot."

"Are there any available spaces around any of our gyms?"

"Not all of them, but one for sure has a lot on the opposite side of it. I already put a bid down."

"Good. I think we should make it free for our gym for up to five hours and we should charge for overnight stay for the rest of the residents."

"Maybe give a discounted rate for overnight parking if our gym members need it." Tone suggested.

We started talking more about business

and it was good. It took my mind off of Jayla and the situation with my baby mother. It was nice not to worry about her crazy ass popping up and doing stupid shit again.

"You okay?" Tone asked me.

"I'm good, why did you ask?"

"Because I've been talking about the business and you got this look on your face like someone pissed in your lemonade."

"I'm just thinking."

"I can tell. What you thinking about? Let me guess, Jayla?"

"Yeah, but really Damiah."

"Oh, damn."

Tone knew about all the drama I'd had with my baby momma. He'd seen and heard all the shit she'd put me through.

"What she's done now?" He grabbed another beer out the fridge. "She go on your Facebook and tried to see who has been in your inbox?" He chuckled, remembering something that happened in my past.

"She popped up on Jayla."

"At her house?"

"At her job." I shook my head.

"That bitch is crazy," he muttered. "No disrespect."

"Don't worry about that because I agree with you."

"How the fuck she even find out where Jayla works? Or how did she even know who she is?"

"I don't know." I shrugged.

"I wouldn't put it past if she was stalking you. Remember how she use to go crazy for the randoms you use to run through?" he reminded me.

"What do you mean?"

"Oh come on Shane, you have to be smarter than that. You didn't think it was weird that you would have some chick at your house, and she just pop up out of nowhere? I can see it now. Her crazy ass in the car watching your ass with some binoculars." He laughed.

"It's not that funny."

"Nah it ain't, it's sad."

Tone was right. I was sick and tired of Damiah's drama. Knowing what she did to Jayla still pissed me off to this day. She could have ruined a great thing for me. I just hoped that telling her the whole truth and us slowing down could help us in the long run.

"Well, I'm going to call it a night." I gave Tone a dap. "Keep my guest room clean."

"What is that supposed to mean?" Tone laughed.

"Keep all your young thots out that room."

CHAPTER 4

Jayla

"Where are you going?" Keon asked me with his arms crossed. He was standing by the doorway.

"Excuse me?" I crossed my arms back at him. "Do you think that you are my Dad or something?" I laughed at my little brother. "Why are you here acting crazy?"

"I'm just curious about where you're going." He chuckled.

"Just out with—"

"Shane." My brother cut me off. "Okay, be safe."

I was about to tell him off again, but I

knew he wanted the best for me. I just waved goodbye to him and hopped in the ride that Shane sent over. Once again, he was surprising me with another date. It had been a while since our last date because our schedules got so crazy. It was weird; Shane and I been on a lot of dates, but every time I went to go meet with him, I got nervous. It almost always felt like the first date all over again.

"Here we are," the driver said and I looked up.

"Are you sure that we're at the right place?" I was confused and I took out my phone.

"I'm positive."

"No, this has to be a mistake." I went to text Shane but then he came up to the window. "I guess this wasn't a mistake."

Stepping out the car, the wind hit me hard. Before I could bundle up, Shane took off his jacket and put it on my shoulders. I smiled at him.

"I might be underdressed." I was wearing a top with a short skirt.

"I know that you're use to a fancy restaurant but I just wanted to hang out with you."

He gestured towards the place. It was a small diner and not what I expected at all.

"It was a little shocking but honestly, as long as I get to hang out with you, I'm fine."

We went inside the diner and ordered some pancakes and eggs. After the waitress poured us our cups of coffee, I nudged Shane on the shoulder.

"What's up? You seem like you have a lot on your mind." I saw him holding his cup of coffee and was barely looking at me.

"I do." He sighed. "Samara told me what happened the other day."

"What happened? I don't understand what you mean."

"She told me that she told you a little bit about our past."

"Yeah." I sipped the coffee. "She didn't tell me much but now I feel like I understand you more."

"That's good, but I think you should hear the rest." He looked dead in my eyes.

I felt this weight on my shoulders. Suddenly the whole diner went silent even though I knew it really wasn't. I just wanted to hang on to every word he was going to say.

When Samara told me that there were some things that only Shane could tell me, I was worried, but I never had the courage to ask him.

"I know she told you that we didn't have the best growing up, and that's all true. Samara and I couldn't rely on any of the adults, so I had to provide for Samara myself. I tried to do some odd end jobs, you know construction, pick up trash, but none of that paid. I couldn't be broke for that long so naturally I fell into what I could. I started drug dealing."

My heart dropped. It wasn't what I expected to hear, but I guess I understood.

"And I made a lot of money drug dealing. I made enough money for Samara and me. I could pay the rent, I could buy her clothes, I could watch out after her. It was so nice to provide for once. We went from struggling to making it. Then something happened."

"What happened?"

"I started to change."

The waitress came with our pancakes and eggs. I ordered some turkey bacon and some orange juice.

"How did you change?"

"I started to make a lot of money. I started to make more money than I ever have before. It was nice. I started to be able to have almost anything I wanted. I could snap my fingers and I would have it. I was starting to become greedy. I was starting to be careless and if I did care, I was only caring about money. I didn't like who I was becoming. I liked being successful, but not like that. So I left the game. I took all the money that I had and focused on legit businesses and school. I learned about how to run a franchise and how to be a businessman. I didn't want drug dealing to be my career anymore, and it was the best decision I ever made."

I digested everything he was telling me.

"So you did what you had to do." I started to speak. "I can understand that." I nodded. "My parents were unreliable."

"How?"

"My mom had a bad habit and my father…" I let the sentence drop.

"What about your father?"

"He was a drug dealer." I looked in his eyes.

It was silent again. The tension made it hard to move. I finally got the courage to look into his eyes. They were understand but a little bit sad.

"So I'm guessing you know something about the drug game?" he asked after he chuckled.

"Yeah I do. I can understand how someone can get into it because they want to provide a better life for their family. As bad as it is, the drug money put a lot of food into our stomachs and clothes on our backs. I can't say that I'm completely mad about it, but after it cost my father his life, I steer clear away from it and anyone who is in the game." I was honest with him.

"Growing up on the streets of Chicago was tough. After my father was killed my mother basically checked out. All she cared about was getting drunk or high. Seeing her turn into a ghost, I had to step up and take care of my brother and sister. I had to become the mom so quick. I bust my ass so hard and now that both of my siblings are in college, I'm so happy. I'm at a point that I don't even get tired anymore because I see how good they both are doing. I will do anything for my brother and sister."

He nodded his head. I felt closer to him when I told him the story. Not only because I was holding it back, but I knew he would be one of the few people that would understand when I spoke about working hard for your siblings. He knew firsthand how it was to go from sibling to parent within a blink of an eye.

"Wow." He finally spoke after some time. "I see we have a lot more in common than we ever thought." He grinned.

"I guess so." I smiled right back at him.

"So, tell me about your last relationship," he asked and I froze. I didn't know why it threw me off when he asked me, especially since he told me more about his baby mother. It only seemed fair that I tell him more about Darius.

"My last relationship...wasn't perfect," I started slowly.

"No relationship is perfect," he added.

"Well this one was far from perfect. He was nice and sweet but he was a liar. He had this whole thing going on and we were so rocky and tumultuous. It was a lot of back and forth and finally we got to a place where everything was going to be ok. He was working hard for us to get together. It looked like everything was going to be okay, but then things went left. He was murdered and that was it."

Just then the waitress walked over. She gave me a look and tried to pretend that she didn't just hear what I said. She gave me my extra helping of bacon. I slid the plate closer to Shane so that he could have some pieces. He took one and chewed it slowly… or maybe it wasn't that slow. Maybe I was just so anxious for a reaction from him. Every second that he didn't say anything felt like an hour.

"I'm sorry to hear that. It sounds like a lot to go through."

"It was." I nodded. I blinked my eyes because I didn't want to start crying in the middle of this diner. "And that's why I'm here. I had to leave Atlanta and have a fresh new start. I got me and my brother here and we haven't looked back."

"And I'm glad that you did. Hearing how he changed his life around shows that you made the right choice. You should be proud of that."

"And all that bullshit with the relationship is why I'm not rushing into another one," I confessed.

"I understand and I'm willing to wait," he told me. He held my face with one of his hands. "You're worth the wait. I appreciate the kind of woman you are Jayla, and you need to know, I'm not going anywhere."

He kissed my forehead and I smiled back at him. I tried to keep it cool, but inside I felt it happening. I looked in his eyes and that's when I knew. I was falling for him.

CHAPTER 5

Jayla

"Keon!" Crystal yelled. "Are you going to help us with breakfast or are you just going to take your time?" She rolled her eyes and looked over at me. "Jayla, I'm not going to do it. I'm not going to start cooking breakfast because he's taking so long. I know that's his plan. He wants me to get tired of waiting for him and then I'm going to end up cooking breakfast. Nope, I'm not doing that this time no matter how long he takes." She pouted and I laughed. My brother and his girlfriend always cracked me up. I knew that sometimes that my brother got Crystal to cook somehow, but I hope that this time it wasn't true because he promised French toast.

"You're always whining." He walked in, rubbing his eyes. "I just wanted to make sure that I washed up before I started. I mean, you don't want me cooking with morning breath, do you?" He blew air in our faces. "See? Minty fresh!" He smiled and we both laughed. "Okay let me get started on the French toast and bacon."

"Ugh, I've had enough bacon." I remembered the diner.

"How can one have enough bacon?" Crystal asked. "I don't think that is physically possible."

"Well last night me and Shane ate a whole bunch of bacon."

"Oooh, Shane." Crystal's eyes lit up.

Crystal loved to hear stories about me and Shane. She really was likc a sister so it never felt weird to tell her.

"Yes, I went on another date with Shane."

"Good." She smiled. "What happened? Did you guys finally—"

"Before you continue…" Keon cut her off, "I'd like to remind you that her little brother is in the room. So please keep all the conversa-tions...clean." He warned us and we shook our heads.

"What I was going to say is did you guys commit to each other. You have to be more than just dating or just trying things out. It's been forever."

"It hasn't been forever."

"Please Jayla, ya moving at the speed of slugs or something." Keon laughed.

"Don't say that." Crystal joined in on the laughter. "Maybe they are just getting to know each other. You know that takes some time," she added.

"Well I did get to know some things about him."

I then went on to tell them a little bit of what Shane told me. I didn't go too much into detail because it really wasn't my story to share. When I finished, I looked over at the both, but mostly at Keon. He knew just like I did about the street life. In fact, he may know more than I do because he was a little into the life too

"What are you thinking about, Keon?" I wondered.

"I'm thinking that this Shane guy is a good dude. He hasn't done anything so far that makes me feel like I need to choke him out." He shrugged his shoulders. "I like him, but I just see how you are and I'm thinking you can do more. I know a thing or two about dudes and the fact that he's not trying to get into your drawers, that says a lot."

"I thought we weren't supposed to talk about my sex life?" I asked.

"Whatever. I'm just wondering why you're taking your time with him," Keon asked.

"I just want to take things slow with him." I took a bite into the French toast. It was surprisingly good. I guess cooking was another thing that Crystal had taught Keon.

"And I think that's cool. I think that you should do that, but damn give that dude a chance. You got to feel him out and see how it goes. You deserve love Jayla. I keep telling you this, but stop letting what happened with Darius fuck up what you have now. You came here for a new life and you are letting your past life stop you. You deserve more than this. You are here for a new life, so live that life."

Crystal went up and hugged Keon.

"That was so sweet for you to say to your sister." She kissed his cheek. "And he's right, Jayla. You keep trying to have your guard up, but you're always going out with him, and you're always talking about him. You're so into Shane. You are all about him, even if you don't see it. You are letting your past hinder your future."

I agreed with them. Once again, they were right. We ate breakfast and talked about a lot of things, but I was not really listening. I kept hearing what they just told me again in my head. Pretty soon breakfast was done and they were gone. They were going to spend the whole day together and I just wanted to really think about what I was doing with Shane. I climbed back into bed and thought about it. How would life be if I really let my guard down and put myself all out there for Shane? What if I didn't let Darius hold me back? What if his baby momma learned her place? What if we could beat the odds and be something real? What if? What if?

CHAPTER 6

Damiah

"Bitch, if you don't chug that Henny you ain't a real bitch!" my bestie, Brit, told me.

"Girl, no one fucking chugs Henny," I giggled. "I'll take another shot though. Pour it up." She filled up my shot glass and I threw it back.

"That's right, take it like a motherfucking G," she joked.

Me and my bestie Britanya were wasted. We started with the clear water but soon we got to drinking the brown water like always. After I dropped my son off, I knew that I had to send a message to my friend for us to get super drunk. I'd been having a rough couple of days and only hard liquor would solve it. So, me and Brit started with beers and now we were finishing off the hard shit.

"I can't believe all this bullshit," I started to tell Brit.

"What bullshit?" she looked over at me and asked.

"I'm talking about my man Shane trying to be with some new bitch. He really out here trying to move on. He knows, like everybody knows, that I'm the woman that he is meant to be with. I could get it if he was just going to fuck this girl and throw her away, but he is actually claiming her. He called her his girl. What type of fucked up shit is that?" I shook my head and took a sip of the Henny. "That's not right."

"She's just this fucking gold digger anyway." Brit was right as always. "She's going to be fucking and sucking him until she can get all the money."

"All of his money!" I agreed. "I ran up on the chick at the job...that ole scary chick." I started laughing remembering what happened when I went to her job. "That bitch didn't try to swing or fight me back. She not about this life. She not about what me and Shane can do. She really thinks that she is somebody."

"She probably pissed her pants when she saw you." Brit laughed and I started cracking up.

"She probably did. I'm just mad I didn't get to fuck her up the way I wanted. Her stupid co."

"There will always be another time, or are you going to listen to what Shane told you to do? Are you going to leave her alone?"

Out of nowhere, I saw Shane's face again. I heard his warning and I damn near felt it the way he had his hand around my neck. He meant business, but Shane was my true love and I was his. We had been together for too long for us to turn around and just end it. And we were ending it for some chick? Straight bullshit. How could he forget everything just because he got with some girl?

"Shane is such a fucking lame. I can't wait to be there when his dumbass find out that she just wants his money. I can't wait to see him come back to me begging and telling me that I was right about this chick. I can't wait for that day. He really thinks her lame ass is better than me. When she takes all of his money, he's gonna find out how much better I am than her. He really ain't shit. He gonna be there looking so fucking stupid and my petty ass is just going to laugh. I'm going to tell him about himself but because we are meant to be together, I'm going to forgive him."

Brit nodded her head and we saw that the bottle was done. She tried to stand up but she sat right back down.

"A bitch is fucked up!" she laughed as she fell to the couch again. She kept trying to get up but eventually gave up. "But don't worry about Shane." She turned to me.

"Why not?"

"Shane is a fucking lame," she told me. "He got one of the baddest bitches out there and he want to settle down with a basic bitch. Let them two run off and be basic together. Better yet, I hope that basic bitch does take all his money and leaves his dumb ass."

"Yeah." I nodded.

"I never really liked his dumb ass anyway."

"Yeah..." I could feel the tears coming.

Fucking drinking Henny always got me emotional and shit.

"You alright?"

That was when I lost it. When Brit asked me that, I just started to sob out loud. I buried my face into my hands and just let all the tears fall. This hurt, this really fucking hurt. All this time I spent with Shane, all of these years, all of the happy moments, everything was now gone. How could it be over? How could we be done? How could he just be finished with me? I thought we were supposed to last forever. How was that just gone? How did forever turn into this?

"Are you okay?" Brit asked me.

"No, I'm not okay!" I cried. "I love that man and he's acting like he's done with me. Shane is the love of my fucking life and he doesn't seem to care. The way he is with this chick, it's almost like I don't even exist. It's like I don't fucking matter Brit." I sniffled. "It was like just yesterday that man loved me. He loved to take me out, he loved to take me shopping, and he used to make me laugh like crazy. You don't make that type of connection with just anyone. You don't just fall in love and fall right out of it. That's not how this shit works. He was there for me. He was my rock. Shane is my everything!" I sobbed louder.

Brit hugged and started rubbing my back. I started to calm down, but just thinking about Shane made me like this.

"I know that you love him and I know that you two had something special. You guys were really in love and that's how you got your son. I know you think that he is your soulmate and that things were good at one time, but right now…" She didn't finish her sentence. I could hear her taking a slow breath. "But what you are going through right now just shows that it's not good anymore. It seems to be a lot on you and doing a lot to you. This relationship isn't good." She stated again. "Whatever it is or was, is done."

I cried even more. My heart felt like it was going to beat out of my chest. I tried to breathe deeply. This pain that I was feeling was like nothing that I ever felt before. The shit was driving me crazy.

"I know it hurts but you have to move on and find a man that's going to treat you better. You got to stop being stuck on stupid on

Shane. You can do better the only way that can happen is when you leave his dusty ass alone for good. And a bad bitch like you, you are going to bad a real nigga. That new nigga gonna be paid, treat you nice, and dusty ass Shane gonna be feeling stupid."

I nodded my head but I didn't agree with Brit. She didn't know what she was talking about. It was easy for her to say that I should leave Shane alone because she wasn't going through the same process I was. She couldn't understand it, no matter how hard she tried. She could mention a new guy, but that didn't matter. I was in love with Shane and I would probably always be in love with him. It's not easy to shake off your true love; not at all.

CHAPTER 7

Shane

"Okay, now we're going to make sure that the juice bar is up and running from 5 in the morning to about 8 in the evening. I think the morning rush from the early birds that come to work out will bring in a lot of money for the juice bar area." Tone and I were in my office going over the new plans we have for all our locations.

"Yeah. I think we should roll out some new promotion for that. There is no point of having this juice bar if no one knows about it." He took out his phone. "I'm going to send out an email to our marketing team and see what ideas they have for that. I'm thinking maybe pay a few fitness gurus to talk about it."

"Only ones that are based in Houston," I added. "There's no need to spend money on fitness celebs that are never really in Houston. We need Houston based fitness social media stars, or at least ones who are very active in Houston."

"Do you offer them free memberships?"

"I guess so, but they have to get paid. Free memberships are not enough, especially since our prices can range from inexpensive to really expensive. With this endorsement we can't be cheap. Whoever we pick, we have to cut them a decent check. Nothing to make them retire but something to make them really promote our gym on a great day-to-day basis."

Tone and I went back and forth talking about ways we could expand our business. We successfully launched a new gym. The gym brought in so many new members and three celeb clients. Our trainers implemented this new training program and now that we had a bar serving hot food, it even included a meal plan. Everyone was talking about it and the gym even got a feature on a well-known fitness blog. We were doing real well and I should have been crazy happy about the success, but as much as I tried not to, I was thinking about Jayla.

She was a different type of woman. Just the way she carried herself showed me that. She was still making sure that we didn't rush into anything. She never asked me for money, she never asked for anything, and now knowing that we practically grew up the same way, some things started to make sense. She and I had so much in common that it was getting scary. I would have never looked at her and guessed her past. The other thing was that she never carried around her past like a burden. She never was hard or mean to everybody else because of what she went through. She really was one of a kind.

"Alright, I think we pretty much know what we're going to do." Tone started to stand up. He was obviously trying to end this meeting. He was staring at his phone with a slick smile on his face.

"And where are you going?" I asked, but I already had my suspicions.

"Nothing." He wasn't even looking at me.

He was staring at his phone and still had that goofy ass grin on his face. "I'm just going to do something real quick."

"What's her name?"

"What do you mean?" He was trying to sound innocent but I knew him better than that. Tone and I went way back, so I knew before he said anything.

"Come on Tone, this is me you're talking to. I know if you staring at your phone like that...I know what that means."

"Nigga, you don't know me," he joked.

"Yeah, right." I laughed. "What you getting into? Or who you getting into? I know that you talking to some chick."

"Briana." His eyebrows jumped up and down. "She got a twin sister if you're interested."

"Nah, I'm good."

"Let me guess, you're still on Jayla." He shook his head. "Guess I'll have to have them all to myself," he said, and he was out.

I chuckled, thinking about Tone. He was serious when he said he was not going to settle down. To be honest, it wasn't that long ago that I was the same. After Damiah and all that shit she put me through, the last thing I was thinking about was getting serious with another female. I didn't want that at all but here I was, thinking about Jayla.

Without noticing it, I started to call Jayla. I didn't mean to, but I just went for my phone and started dialing her number.

"Hello?" Her voice made me smile a little.

"Jayla, how are you?"

"I'm fine Shane. How are you?" She was joking, being very formal with me.

"I'm well, thank you for asking. I was actually calling you to see if you'd like to go out tonight."

"Of course. Where are we going, or are you going to surprise me as always?"

"I don't know." I grinned. "Maybe."

"How about we just go out for drinks?" she suggested. "I had a long day at work and a couple of drinks would be nice right about now."

"Was it a bad day?"

"Not the greatest." She sighed. "Drinks would really hit the spot."

"Then how about I pick you up at 8 and we'll go from there?"

"Sounds perfect."

After we set the date, the rest of the day flew by. I didn't know if time was running faster or was it that I was so excited to hang out with Jayla. After I wrapped up all my work, I went home and got ready.

"Yo, I'm out." Tone knocked on my bedroom door. "The floors are finished and everything is done." He leaned on my door frame. "You no longer have a roommate." He gave me a toothy grin.

"I guess not." I went to my closet and started pulling clothes out.

"You on your way out or something?"

"Yeah, just getting ready to go see Jayla. I'm going to pick her up and then we're going to get some drinks."

"You forgot the part of when you come home and beat your meat because you still not getting any."

"Ha ha." I laughed sarcastically. "I will not. I'll just come home and do some work, like I always do."

"Whatever." He chuckled. "I'm not going to be here anyway. You can come home and beat your meat all night long!"

It was 8 o'clock and I was ringing Jayla's doorbell. When she opened the door, I was stunned. This woman was just gorgeous. Her hair, her face, that sexy red dress, her shoes...it was all perfect.

"Wow," I said out loud but I didn't mean to.

"Thank you." She blushed. She looked me up and down and smiled. "You look great too." I smiled back at her and she blushed even more. "Should we get going?"

I brought her to the Grand Prize Bar. It was a well-known spot in Houston. It had a pretty cool vibe, great bar games, and the drinks were some of the best I ever had.

"I've heard of this place, but I've never had the chance to come here." Jayla looked around the bar. "It's nice."

"Yeah, it's not so far from University of Houston. So sometimes it might be crowded with kids from college or just people in general."

"Is that why you parked your car at that lot?"

"Yeah, I just paid for overnight because it's cheaper than paying by the hour. By the way you were sounding on the phone call it seemed like we might be here for a while."

"Yes." She sighed. "I need to relax. Just—" She took in a deep breath. "Let's get started."

We started drinking right away. The second we got to the bar, Jayla ordered us both a round of shots. I was surprised, but figured her day was really weighing down on her. As she finished with the shots, she ordered a peach martini.

"You weren't kidding when you said that you needed a drink or two."

"I really wasn't." She threw back her martini. "Now don't make me look like a drunk. Come on, have some drinks with me."

"I guess it's a good thing that I paid for overnight parking. Looks like I'll be taking an Uber home." I chuckled and signaled the bartender over.

"Play your cards right and I might be going with you." She gave me a sexy side eye and ordered another martini. "But just to make sure you get into your house safe." She had a wicked smile on her face. "Purely innocent, I assure you."

"I'm sure."

After a few more drinks, I felt a little buzz and I tried to keep my cool, but when Jayla accidentally pushed against me, I said something I never expected to.

"You're so fucking sexy." The words came out of me so quickly. I shook my head slightly because I didn't mean for it to come out like that. "I'm sorry, I guess——"

'It's okay." She laughed. "You're just being honest. If that's how you feel then I can't blame you. "

"I can blame that dress you're wearing." I felt a little bit bolder now.

"You like my dress?" She spun around and showed off her figure. "What do you like about it? Is it the fact that it's short? Or how about the fact that it's backless?"

"Yes, all of the above," I groaned.

"Well I like this blazer you're wearing." She touched my blazer and pressed against my chest. "It's a very nice fit." I could feel her purposely touching my chest muscles. Then her hand went down further to touch my abs. "This shirt is pretty nice too."

I took a step back because I remembered we were trying to take it slow, but she was making it so hard...literally and figuratively. Her perfume, her look, and the way that she was looking at me wasn't making it easy.

"What happened?" she asked but she knew; she had to know.

"Just needed to take a step back," I chuckled, looking directly into her eyes.

"It's a good thing you did. I would have touched a little bit more." She inched a little closer to me.

"It's a good thing that I can't touch you."

"Who says that you can't?"

"Is this your way of saying that I have permission?"

I couldn't remember what happened, but I just remembered throwing some money down at the bar, flagging a cab down, and us taking it back to my place. The whole time in the back of the cab we were all over each other. It happened so fast, I didn't know who made the first move. It was like we both just went for each other. I started kissing her lips but we were so into it, I moved on to kissing her neck. She moaned and then pulled me off of her. Then she kissed me back and went to kiss my neck. She started biting on it and I damn near lost my mind. I took a deep breath and let her do whatever she wanted.

"Damn, you don't know how bad I want you," I told her truthfully.

"I want you too." She kissed me soft and long. I let my hands roam her entire body. She felt even better than I ever could have imagined. She was so beautiful and felt so soft. When she pulled me in tighter for a kiss, her whole smell just grabbed ahold of me. This woman had got my attention.

The cab stopped in front of my place. The cabbie barely made eyes at me but I didn't care. I didn't bother asking him how much it was. I just threw $50 at him and me and Jayla got out of the car.

"So this is it," I said, because I kind of expected her to walk away. We both agreed to take it slow but there was something in the air tonight. Something was so different right now. Suddenly both of us seemed to not give a fuck about all the rules that we set for ourselves. We just wanted each other. I wanted to make sure that we were still on the same page though. The last thing I wanted to do was rush her into anything that she wasn't ready for.

"Take me inside," she said flat out, and I listened.

I brought her in my place. Just as I was about to show her around, she grabbed me in for a kiss. I walked her against the wall and kissed her strongly again. I grabbed her whole body and pulled it against me. She started moaning into my ear.

"You don't know how bad I want you to fuck me," she confessed, and hearing her say those words shocked me. She kissed me again and then pulled my blazer off of me. I lifted my shirt off and she passed her hands on my chest. "You just have no idea."

"So, you're still touching me?" I asked. She bit her bottom lip and nodded slowly.

"Why haven't you touched me yet?" she asked.

"I did a little touching." I kissed her again. I didn't want to tell her that I was afraid if I started touching her, I wouldn't be able to stop.

"Why don't you touch me the way you really want to?"

"Are you sure about this?" I asked. I didn't know why I felt the need to make sure that she was up to this, but I did. I didn't want her doing anything that she didn't want to. She smirked and then kissed me deeply.

"Yes, Shane." Her eyes twinkled. "I want you to really touch me. You can touch me any way you want."

"That's all I needed to hear."

I lifted her up and she wrapped her legs around me. Squeezing her thighs and ass, she moaned and kissed me again. I walked over to my desk and pushed everything to the ground. I kissed her neck and her body moved up. She moaned as I bit her neck and then placed my hands in between her legs. She was so warm, wet, and perfect. I kissed her deeply and let my hands explore her whole body. I felt every part of her, all the curves, all her softness, and I felt excited. It was like waiting for a gift for so long and now I finally got my chance. I just wanted to take my time. Every time I kissed her, I took my time. When I touched her, I took a little bit longer because I just wanted to enjoy it.

"Damn, baby," she moaned. She was grabbing on me and pulling on me. She wanted to kiss me again and I did too.

"You want another kiss?" I asked and she nodded. "Good, I've been waiting on this." I opened her legs and kiss her lips nice and soft. Her whole body shot up but she managed to dig my head in deeper. I ran my tongue everywhere while paying attention to how her body reacted. If she moaned in pleasure, I licked there a lot faster or slower. I tongue kissed her lower lips and she covered me with herself. She took in deep breaths, started to quiver, and kept trying to speak but nothing came out.

The whole desk shook as she did. She came up to me and grabbed me in for a kiss. I lifted her off the desk and she slid out of my arms and got on her knees. She pulled my pants down quickly and I pulled her up for another kiss. She was kissing down my chest. When she looked up at me, I smirked. She pulled my boxers off and went to work. I rolled my head back. She did this thing with her tongue that almost made me fall to my knees. She was taking the soul right out of me and I couldn't even grasp how she could be this good. I held her head and before I knew it, I finished.

She came up and took off her dress. I stared at her whole body for a quick second but I just wanted to have at her. With that, we went at each other. Somehow we ended up on the floor. I was on my back and she was on top of me. She danced and moved so well and sexy on me. She grinned at me as she passed her hand down my chest. She grabbed ahold of my manhood. I was rock hard at this time and I didn't know where she was going with this. She just looked at me in a way that was so seductive and then put me inside of her slowly. I took in a deep breath and just watched her. She started bouncing up and down, licking her lips, and riding me like crazy. Her hips moved in ways that I never thought possible. She leaned over and kissed me.

"You like that?" she asked and then clenched on me.

"You think this is a game?" I chuckled and started moving in and out of her. "I'm going to win this."

We flipped over and I was on top of her. We moved together at the same time. I was hitting all her spots, because she was screaming like crazy. She dug her nails into my back and bit her lip. I swirled my hips and pulled out a little.

"What are you doing?" she gasped. "Please don't stop," she whispered, and then I put myself all the way back inside of her. She chuckled slowly. "You're so bad," she groaned.

We were everywhere and all over the place. We got to the bedroom but we never got to the bed. We fucked on the couch, the table, my chair, everywhere. I'd never had it like this. It was weird for it to be this good, but it was so great. It was like we'd been fucking for years and we had learned each other bodies. How was it that she knew the shit I liked without me saying a word?

I kissed her forehead. We were done and I was finally catching my breath. I pulled her close to me and hugged her tight.

"I've wanted that for so long." I held her and played with her hair. "But I didn't think it was going to be that good. Don't get me wrong, I knew it was going to be good—great, even, but damn that shit was much better than I ever expected." I kissed her again and she smiled. She sighed but then her eyes looked away. She was getting really silent. It felt kind of weird. "Is everything okay?" I asked her.

"I shouldn't be here."

She then pulled away from me. I reached out for her again, but she was out of my grasp. She got up and started to walk away. I was confused.

"What?" I got up after her. "Jayla, what's going on?"

"I got to get out of here."

"Wait, what? I don't get what's going on." I went after her but she was grabbing her clothes. As fast as her clothes flew off, she was throwing it back on even quicker. She pulled out her phone and started to really leave. She was going so fast that I could barely put on my boxers and shirt.

"I just got to go."

She was by the front door when I caught up to her.

"What's going on, Jayla? I thought everything was okay, I thought it was great, but I don't understand this." I tried to look into her eyes but she was avoiding me. I had to get ahold of the situation.

"It's not you." She was trying to leave but I held on to her hand.

"Talk to me. Tell me what's going on."

"It's nothing." She was still trying to go but I need an answer. Everything was going great, and then suddenly...

"Stay here, let's talk about it."

"It's nothing, Shane." She smiled at me but I didn't believe it. She was still avoiding my eyes. "I just have to get ready for work."

"Are you sure it's about work? Is there anything we should talk about?" I finally got her to look at me. She was trying to look like everything was cool, but her eyes said something else. I was not sure what it was saying, but I knew something changed.

"Shane, it's work." She was trying to convince me but didn't believe it. I tried to say something else, but she opened up her mouth first. "It's okay, Shane. It's nothing really. I just have to get up early tomorrow morning for work. I just want to get home so I can do that."

"Jayla—"

"Bye."

She was out before I could say anything

else or even do anything else. I opened the door and she was already walking down the block. I went after her. I was about to offer to give her a ride home but that wasn't necessary. A car pulled up, she flagged it down, and was gone. I watched her leave.

"Fuck!" I shouted. What just happened? What did I do? I thought that we were on the same page, and now I was not so sure.

CHAPTER 8

Jayla

The Uber ride home was calm but my heart was racing. I couldn't believe what just happened. How could this have happened? How did it even start? I just remembered we were at the bar and next thing I knew, we were back in his crib. One minute we were just having fun and then our clothes just flew off of us. He touched me in a way I didn't even know my body enjoyed, but I was still in shock. It was all so good, a little bit too good.

His hands were still over me, but I couldn't believe I gave in to the feeling. The sex was amazing, outstanding, and was better than I even fantasized that it could be, but that could mean one thing: cloudy vision.

Great sex is so intoxicating while you're doing it. I swear the whole time I could feel myself getting drunk and high off of Shane. I didn't want to stop. I didn't want him to stop. I wanted the sex to last forever and ever. One touch and I had to keep on touching him. One taste and I had to keep going. One stroke...and I had to feel him even more. I felt parts of my body awaken in a way I never expected. It really took me for a loop, but I knew that all of this could make me become blind to certain things. Good dick can make a sister Stevie Wonder blind to a lot of bullshit, and I didn't want that to happen.

I loved Darius from the bottom of my heart. I truly did. He was so nice to me and the sex was so great, which was why he may have been able to get away with a lot of bull-shit. If the D wasn't so good, I would have probably put two and two together. I would have known about his wife and his kid, had the sex not blinded me to so much. Now that I thought about it, every time I even thought about leaving, we would have sex and then we became okay. That cannot happen with Shane, especially with his crazy ass baby mama.

Honestly, I hadn't even wrapped my head around the thought of dating someone with a kid, let alone someone with a kid and a crazy baby mama. Not to be negative, but I never wanted to date a man with a kid. It was nothing to do with him really. I didn't want a man to feel like he would ever have to choose between me and his kid. When a father doesn't live with the child, he doesn't get a lot of time with them. His time that he gets with his kid is precious and I would never want to come in between that. It's just a lot to take on a man with a kid and I didn't think I am ready for, but what about Shane? He was making me rethink this rule of mine. Could he be worth it?

Shane was nice and he was really sweet. He treated me great and even better than

Darius did. Once everything was out in the open, I felt like I could trust him more and more. We had so much in common and we just connected. In so many ways, Shane could be the perfect guy for me, but of course, there was one problem. And it's not like the one problem was small. It was huge and could break us up. The one problem being his baby mama. I told myself once I came out to Houston that I wanted no parts of any type of drama. Shane was cool and I could even accept and later love his kid, but his baby mama? I didn't know if I wanted to deal with that in the long run.

I liked the way that my life is right now. There was hardly ever drama and I was having a great time. I had a great job, my brother turned his life around, and everything seemed to be falling into place. I didn't know if I could continue to do that if I dated Shane. A man with a child is a lot of baggage honestly. Everybody comes with their own set of baggage, whether it's trust issues, cheating issues, or whatever, but when you come with a child, you have to deal with their issues, as well as this whole new family. You have to respect the child and the family that your man has with the baby mother. Could I really do that with his baby mama just popping up where she wasn't wanted? Maybe if his baby mama was somebody I could respect or someone that knew her place, this whole situation could be easier to take. If Damiah was cool, this whole thing would be smooth sailing, but this wasn't the case. She was a person that didn't seem to have a problem butting into Shane's business, and I didn't think I should have to deal with that.

Laying down in bed, I was waiting for sleep to come to me, but it was nowhere near. My head was racing and going crazy from all that happened today. I wanted to be tired and I thought by the time I climbed into bed, I would have passed out, but my thoughts were still driving me crazy. Should I stick it out with Shane? Should I just go? Was I really ready to be dealing with his kid and his baby momma? I guess the real question was, was I willing to let Shane go? I didn't even have to think about that one. I was falling for Shane and even with all of this, I couldn't see myself letting him go. To give him credit, he did handle the situation with his baby momma. I hadn't seen her at all, so I should give him his chance. Keon was always telling me to stop holding back on Shane, and he was right. I had to give him a shot and see where Shane and I could go.

CHAPTER 9

His POV

I flung the ad for the brand new gym opening across the room. It was like every time I turned around, there was another ad for this fucking gym. Look at Shane in all his mother-fucking glory. He's really a piece of shit. He ruined my life and he's managed to make money in the process. I'd known Shane his whole life. I'd practically watched him grow up. I saw everything and I knew everything, and that motherfucker thought he's better than me. He thinks that his fancy cars, nice house, his fucking gyms made him the man, but it didn't make him shit. He knew it and I knew it too.

The bottle of Hennessy was almost finished, but I downed it all like it was full. I went to the cabinet and looked for another one. I was feeling too nice to let myself run out of drink. I wanted to keep the feeling going. The cabinet was bare and I just shrugged my shoulders. If I couldn't get even more drink, I would have to do something else to keep me feeling this nice. I pulled out some weed and started to roll it up. Watching it light on fire made me happy every time. It almost did something for me.

"Fucking Shane." I let the smoke travel through my body. It was like medicine hitting me all at once. It was amazing how good this shit felt. It was exactly what I fucking needed after seeing that cheesing ass nigga Shane in that ad. I kept inhaling and puffing and then when I looked down, the weed was gone. I rolled up another one and lit it. The high and the Hennessy was bringing me to feeling lit.

That fucking Shane always thought he was a better man than me. He always thought he was the HNIC, head nigga in charge, but he ain't shit. He was nobody. And I couldn't wait for the world to see it.

Walking around the living room, I thought about Shane and his bitch made ways. He was always trying to do something to show off or flex, but I knew his downfall was coming soon. The thought of Shane down in the gutter made me laugh out loud. I tried to hold back the laughter but as soon as I started there was no stopping it. I was way too fucked up now. I then remembered that I had a small bottle of Henny in a dresser. I ran and found it.

"It's bad enough that he's fucked me over but now he has the woman of my dreams wrapped around his fucking finger." I slammed down the empty bottle of Hennessy on the table. In the corner of my eye, I saw Shane's smile from the ad I threw over. I picked up the bottle and smashed it against the wall. The pieces fell to the floor and the noise echoed throughout the room. "He thinks that's he's on top of the world right now, but just wait. He's going to have to pay what he owes." I finished off my last blunt and blew the smoke in the air. "And there's no escaping that."

CHAPTER 10

Jayla

Waiting on line at the dry cleaners, I looked at the time. I already spent most of my day doing some errands and I still had some more to go. After picking up my newly cleaned uniform for work, I filled up the fridge with groceries, and started cooking some food for Keon and his girlfriend. I was almost finished with cooking when my phone rang.

"Hello Samara," I greeted after seeing her name on my phone's screen. "What's up girl? How are you doing?"

"Hey girl. Are you busy? It's our day off and I was wondering if you were doing anything." There was something off in her voice, but I couldn't put my finger on it.

"No, I was just making some dinner for Keon and his girlfriend. They both have this big exam so I just wanted to do something nice for them. I like to spoil them because they are so nice to me."

"Are you going to eat with them or would you like to go out with me?"

"Of course, girl." I smiled. "I'll meet you for lunch. Text me the details."

"Alright."

We ended the call and I got back finishing the meal for Keon. After I was done, I took a quick shower and got dressed. I met up with Samara at this banging Cajun place. You could smell the food as soon as you entered it. I was a little bit hungry, but it was like the second I could smell the food, I became like a starving person. The waitresses would pass by and I would just start drooling over the food. Samara came in two seconds behind me and her eyes opened wide when she saw all the food. Her eyes followed the waitresses and all the food, just like my eyes were doing.

"Fuck a diet, because we are eating like

pigs today!" she joked and we were soon seated.

After we ordered our drinks and food, I finally got a good look at Samara. She was wearing a sleeveless red dress that hugged her body just right. She paired it with some silver pumps and diamond stud earrings. Samara had always looked good, but today she looked extra nice. She was looking downright sexy.

"Damn girl, had I known that you would have came here looking like this, I would have brought you some flowers or something. Girl, you got me feeling like we on a date on something. You look great!" I complimented her.

"Oh, thank you." She smiled. "And stop lying to yourself." She eyed my whole outfit. "You over here dressed like a cast member of Basketball Wives."

"Oooh bish, which onc?" I joked and we both started laughing. "But seriously, you look really good."

"Thank you again." She squinted at me. "Is this your way of telling me that on those other days I looked like a bum bitch?" She laughed like only she could. Samara always knew how to flip a compliment to something so funny.

"No!" I chuckled out loud. "Never that, but I'm just saying, you look really nice today."

"I guess you can see it," she said quietly while looking around the restaurant.

"See what?" I was confused. I didn't know where she was getting at and I didn't understand it. I don't know why, but I could feel a shift in the conversation.

"I've made a change."

I didn't know what Samara was getting at. I kept trying to think about clues, but nothing came to mind. Maybe something happened with her at the job. I knew she hated the new supervisor. What if she hated the new supervisor so bad that she quit? I didn't know how work would be like without Samara. She brightened up my day when I was at work. She made the day go by much faster and we were always laughing and joking around. What was I going to do if she left the job? What if that was her big change?

"A change? What do you mean by that?" I said slowly because I was honestly afraid of the answer. My mind was getting ahead of myself.

"Well you know my situation with my jail-bird lover." She rolled her eyes slightly.

"I do know your situation, but this is the first time that you've called him that. He was always the love of your life or something like that. Why are you now calling him a jailbird? What happened?"

"What happened was that I took a hard look at my life and I didn't like where it was going."

"Girl, I'm still lost. What are you talking about?"

"I don't want to be chained to some dude in jail."

My jaw nearly hit the table. Here I was worried about work and it wasn't even about that. For as long as I'd known Samara, she'd always been loyal to her man. She was always going on and on about how much she loved him. She talked about her love for him and the family that they shared. She especially spoke about how she was going to stand by him no matter what and wait. What was going on? What had made her change?

"But you always told me that you were going to wait for him and be that ride-or-die chick."

"I don't like my options in that scenario. So it's either I stay out here and be lonely for him or I die? Nah, I'm good." She sighed. "And all this ride-or-die shit is nonsense. Why the woman always got to be the one to ride it out and be perfect while the men can have flaws. I'm over that fucking ride-or-die shit."

"But—"

"I know it's a lot. I know I'm saying a lot of things that seem to be coming out of nowhere." She started to open up. "But to be honest, I got into an argument with him and that's when I really saw what was going on. After we argued I started to see what my life was going to be and I just can't go down that path any longer."

"What was the argument about?"

Samara took a deep breath and I could tell what she was about to say was weighing on her.

"Just stupid shit at first. I thought it was no big deal, but he had to blow the fuck up." She rolled her eyes. "What happened was, I called him like the other day and he flipped on me. I was just venting about how lonely I was out here alone. I missed him and I just wanted him to know that it wasn't easy on me. I wasn't going to do anything and I wasn't even talking to anybody or entertaining, but he swore up and down I was. It's like once I showed him that I was lonely, he automatically was trying to link me with some dick. Jayla, I just wanted to let off some steam, I wasn't even coming at him disrespectfully, but he was telling me that I could never do that. He basically told me that I had to stay to myself and be miserable and it didn't matter what I wanted. I was his and I couldn't be with no one else. He basically started talking about me like I was his property or something."

All this new information was hitting me all at once. Samara never even looked at guys when we went out. Samara was a beautiful girl so naturally men approached her. She would have some great guys approach her, but she never paid them any attention at all. She never flirted with them or even entertained them. She would politely decline them and keep it moving. She had always been loyal to her man and it was kind of sad to see what was happening with them now.

"I get that he's in prison, but him getting caught for doing criminal shit, is not my fault. Why should I be punished too? I feel like I'm in prison too because I can't do anything. I can't live my life. I can't have fun. I am stuck at home with my child while he's in prison telling me to just deal with it." She shook her head. "I don't regret having my son at all, but sometimes I wish I had him in a better situation. I wish I had him where I can have some help."

"I can help babysit. If ever you need some time to yourself you can just leave him with me," I offered.

"I appreciate that, I really do, but it's not enough and it's not your responsibility. I need someone who is going to be there all the time. I'm not saying I'm going to run out and get married now, but the help would be nice."

"I am guessing when you told him all of this, he pictured you running away with some new dude."

"He did!" She took a long sip of her drink. "I just wanted to get some things off of my chest and it didn't go the way I thought it would. After the conversation with him, I'm second guessing a lot of things. I don't think I can do it. I don't think I can be loyal to him if he's being selfish. He's not even thinking about how hard it is on me and our son. He's been in jail for some time that it seems like he's forgotten how it can be out here in the real world. I think I'm done with this, Jayla."

I felt so bad for Samara. I never saw her like this. Just by looking and talking to her, I could tell that she was either giving up or was close to it.

"He keeps telling me that if he finds out that I'm seeing someone, it's going to be a problem." She rolled her eyes and shook her head.

"Can you believe that he would say that to me? I can't believe it especially seeing how I did everything for him and I went above and beyond for him. Like, what the fuck is he going to do to me while he is locked up? He made those mistakes, he chose the streets over me and his son, and now he has to deal with the consequences. I don't know how many times I told him, Jayla, that the streets don't love him. I warned him that if anything happened to him, the streets weren't going to have his back, but he ain't listen to me. Look where he's at right now because he wanted to have more love for the streets than his family. It just doesn't make sense. I got to stay out here and suffer because of his mistakes? I got to be faithful? I got to hold him down? Why should I be faithful to him when he wasn't faithful to me when he was out?"

Samara never mentioned that her baby father was unfaithful. She always said the greatest things about him.

"He was unfaithful?" I asked.

"Typical hood nigga shit. Sells drugs, makes money, and fucks whoever he wants. He started making a little bit of money and making a name for himself in the streets. So you know what happens next, dumb sluts now want to suck his dick and fuck him too. Where were those hoes when he was dead broke? They were nowhere to be found, but as soon as he makes some money, they were all over him." She shook her head again. "And like the typical nigga he was, he fucked them, every chance that he got."

"Wow." She was spilling a lot of tea and it was a lot to take in.

"So, I'm thinking since he's in prison, I'm technically single. He's not around so I'm going to do me."

"Are you saying what I think you're saying?" My eyebrows shot up. "Are you going to start dating?"

"I'm not sure, but I just know I'm not going to be tied down to no jailbird. I'm single."

Lunch with Samara was eye opening to say the least. I couldn't believe what she was going through. During lunch, Samara went on to talk about that she was kind of nervous to start dating. She felt like she would have to start all over again and she wasn't sure how to do it. She had to think about a lot more than I ever did. She had a son to consider and she didn't know how that would factor in her dating life. I gave her the best advice that I could. I couldn't give her any advice on being a single mom. I just suggested to her that she had to be single first before she thought about dating. I told her to not rush into anything and take her time. She just got out of a serious relationship, so the last thing she needed was to jump in another one. She shrugged her shoulders but I think she listened to what I said.

As the sun went down, I made my way back home. I picked up a few things for the house still thinking about my lunch with Samara. She said a whole lot and I couldn't imagine being in her shoes. I hope the best for her and her son. I was about to walk home, I saw something off in the distance. There was someone wearing a dark hoodie walking my way. Before I could do anything, they ran up and grabbed my arm.

"Gotcha bitch!"

Jayla

I can't believe this shit. This bitch had my arm, but I snatched it back from her.

"You got nothing, you crazy bitch!" I turned around and faced her. I pointed my finger in her face. "Don't you ever grab me again!"

"Oh, now you got a little backbone now that you got some of Shane's dick huh? He makes you cum a few times and now you feel like you the baddest bitch in the world? You fucking ho."

"Who the fuck you callin' a ho?"

"You, bitch!" She pointed her finger in my face. "I warned you about staying away from my man, but your dumb ass didn't listen."

Here I was face to face with Shane's baby mother...again. She was dressed in a hoodie and some sneakers. She looked pissed off, but so was I.

"Who the fuck do you think you are?" I asked her.

"Bitch, you know who I am. You know me!" She pointed her finger in my face and I smacked it away. "I'm his fucking future! That's who I am. Don't get confused and think that just because you're fucking him now, that you're important. Don't think that you're going to run off and be his wife. You're not going to be his wife! You're not!" She stepped closer to me.

"Move back, bitch," I warned her. She was getting too close for comfort and I wasn't going to deal with any disrespect this time.

"What?"

"I said move back, bitch."

"Now you want to act all tough and pretend that you're a bad bitch. You're not. I am his wife. I am his love. I am—"

"Shut the fuck up!" I screamed and her eyes opened wide.

Something about her rambling on and on about Shane just made me sick to my stomach. It wasn't even about Shane, but it was about her really believing that her and Shane had a future. I was almost always with Shane, and here she was pretending like I didn't exist.

"I oughtta fuck you up for yelling in my face like that." She looked at me and crossed her arms.

"Go ahead bitch, I'm not at work. I got nothing to lose if me and you go to blows out here." I crossed my arms. "So, what's it going to be?"

"I don't got time to waste."

"Oh, but yes you do bitch." I laughed at the fact she could even say that. "You came here to find me!" I reminded her. "That means you got all the time in the world to waste." I laughed even harder at her stupidity. "You want to talk about you and Shane, but you over here with me. You know it's over between and now you think by getting at me, you're going to have a chance with Shane or something?" I shook my head. "If he wasn't trying to fuck you then…" I sighed. She looked at me and tried to do something. "I wish you would. Give me a fucking reason to lay your ass out on the street"

"You are so dumb." She started laughing out of nowhere. "You really think he's not fucking me?"

Hearing her say those words made my stomach hurt even worse.

"What?" I had to make sure that I heard her right.

"Oh, you're hard of hearing, bitch." She rolled her neck. "Do you think he's not fucking me anymore? When did we stop? We've never stopped fucking," she said slowly.

"You're just saying that to get me mad."

"Bitch, who the fuck are you? Who the fuck are you for me to even care if you're mad or not?"

"I'm the bitch that's on your mind. I'm the bitch that you always popping up to see. So obviously you care about me."

"No, you're the dumb bitch that needs to know the truth. You're the dumb bitch that needs to know her place. You are going to another discarded ho like all the other girls that were dumb enough to think they could ever be me. You're going to be in the past and I'm going to be his future, like we always planned." She smiled and then her smile faded away. "This is going to be the last time that I'm going to warn you. Next time, we're not even going to argue."

"What the fuck is that supposed to mean?"

"Come on, you're not that dumb."

That was when I got mad. I put my hair up in a ponytail and moved even closer to her. We were practically nose-to-nose.

"I don't play with fucking threats, bitch."

"I don't play with them either. I don't just say shit just to say it. I told you once to stay away from him; you should be glad that I am even giving you a second warning. Now leave Shane alone and go about your business." She looked me up and down.

"You're somewhat of a pretty girl, so I'm sure if someone is desperate enough, they'll have you. You might get lucky and find some nigga that has a little bit of coin since that's all you're interested in." She scoffed. "But Shane is mine and will always be mine. He might be telling you that he's single and telling you that me and him are not messing around, but that's the furthest thing from the truth. We are fucking every single night. Every time we meet up, it's all about sex. What? You thought it was just about our son? You thought that he was all about you? Do you think that he's really into you? Don't be dumber than you are." She rolled her eyes.

I didn't know whether or not to believe her, but I knew better than to let her know she had me second guessing Shane.

"Blah, blah, blah." I yawned. "Do you tell those bedtime stories to you or your son? Because it's putting me to sleep, bitch. I mean, this whole fantasy world that you've built up...it's such a great story. You know what you should do? You should write this down and send it to Disney because that's the only way you'll ever get a happy ending. What you're looking for isn't here, hoodrat."

"Hoodrat?"

"Yes. Go on with your life and do hoodrat shit." I rolled my eyes. "I only deal with ladies who have class." I looked her up and down.

She tried to hit me but I moved back.

"Touch me, bitch!" I screamed. "Touch me, bitch! I fucking want you to, you dumb bitch. Put your motherfucking hands on me and see what happens to you."

"Stop that rah-rah mess and go off on me, bitch. You talking all that shit, but when I pressed you at your job you wasn't doing shit. Nothing I hate more than a scary bitch trying to be hard."

"Then go, bitch!" I screamed.

"You want to fight me, bitch!"

"Pop off!"

I don't know when my neighbors came, but they broke us up. My neighbors didn't even get the chance to say anything to Damiah, because she left right after.

"What's going on?" my neighbor asked and I just ignored her. I was pissed off and I didn't know where to start. Not only did Damiah pop back up, but she was saying she was fucking Shane? Was it true? Was he still fucking her? And was Shane worth all this drama?

FIND out what happens next in His Dirty Secret Book 9! Available Now!

FOLLOW Mia Black on Instagram for more updates: @authormiablack